THE BOY WHO CRIED WOLF

Illustrated by Jon Goodell

Adapted by Mary Rowitz

Copyright © 2002 Publications International, Ltd.
All rights reserved. This publication may not be reproduced
in whole or in part by any means whatsoever without written permission from

Louis Weber, C.E.O.
Publications International, Ltd.
7373 North Cicero Avenue
Lincolnwood, Illinois 60712

www.pubint.com

Permission is never granted for commercial

Manufactured in China.

8 7 6 5 4 3 2 1

ISBN: 0-7853-7880-4

There was a young boy who lived in a village. He wasn't very old, but he had an important job. He was a shepherd, and his job was to guard the village's sheep from danger.

The shepherd boy also had to make sure the sheep got plenty of food. Every day he took the sheep to a nearby valley. The villagers trusted him to take good care of the sheep by himself.

The shepherd boy wasn't really all alone. The village people worked nearby. If a wolf ever did attack, the people could run to the rescue.

The villagers counted on the shepherd boy to do his job. They never felt like they had to check on him. They trusted him.

The shepherd watched the sheep from his lookout post. He could also see the people hard at work. Some days they worked at their jobs in the village. Sometimes they did other chores.

For the shepherd boy, every day was the same. He looked at the sheep. They looked the same every day. Then he looked at the forest. It looked the same, too.

In his whole life, the boy had never seen a wolf come near the sheep. In fact, he had never even seen a wolf! Some people told stories of hearing wolves howl in the forest. The boy had never heard any howling. Sometimes he even wondered if there really were any wolves.

One day the shepherd tried to make things more exciting. He thought, "Maybe I can play some games with the sheep." He planned his next day. He smiled when he thought about the fun he would have playing games.

The boy woke up early the next morning. He kissed his parents good-bye and then hurried to take the sheep to the valley. He tried to play games with the sheep. They didn't want to play catch. They weren't interested in trying to  throw the ball. They didn't even want to try to kick the ball. All the sheep wanted to do was eat the grass or take a nap. "This isn't any fun at all," thought the shepherd boy.

The shepherd boy walked slowly back to his lookout post. He could tell the wind was blowing because it made the treetops move. "I wonder," he said, thinking out loud, "what is on the other side of those trees?"

The boy smiled to himself. Would it be so bad to pretend there was a wolf? He thought this would be a good joke.

As the sheep ate the grass, he cupped his hand by his mouth and shouted, "Wolf! Wolf! A wolf is stealing the sheep! Come help me!"

All the village people stopped what they were doing and ran to help scare off the wolf. When they got there, they were very confused.

The villagers did not find a wolf. And where was the shepherd? They were worried about him.

A villager pointed to a tree and said, "There he is over there. Is he okay?" They saw he was not hurt. In fact, he was laughing!

"You looked so funny running up here for no reason. This was a great joke," laughed the boy.

The villagers did not laugh. They had been very frightened for the boy and the sheep. They did not feel like laughing at all. They shook their heads and said, "We have to get back to work now. We don't have time for pranks."

The shepherd boy hardly heard a word they said. He was laughing too hard.

At breakfast the next day, the boy's mother and father told him to be good. He nodded his head and left to tend the sheep. Soon, however, he was bored again. "Wolf! Wolf!" he shouted, louder than the day before. "A wolf is stealing the sheep! Come help me!"

Again the villagers came running. Again there was no wolf in sight. This time the village people were very upset. "If you don't tell people the truth all the time, they will never know when to believe you," they said.

The boy was still laughing at his joke. He did start to think about what they said. "Maybe," he thought, "it isn't so funny to trick people."

On the other side of the trees, a wolf had seen everything. When the shepherd reached his post, the wolf began stealing the sheep. The shepherd couldn't believe it. It was a real wolf! He called out, "Wolf! Wolf! A wolf is stealing the sheep!"

He waited for the villagers to come running. No one did. They weren't going to fall for that trick again! This time, though, it was no trick.

The boy tried yelling for help again, but no one came. He could only watch as the wolf ran off into the forest with all the sheep. This time the only one laughing was the wolf.

The shepherd boy ran into the village. "Wolf! Wolf!" he cried. "He's stealing our sheep!"

"I bet!" said one villager. "I can't believe that boy is trying to make fools out of us again."

"Well, he's not going to make a fool out of me," said another villager. "I don't believe him."

Finally the shepherd boy stopped running. "I'm telling the truth this time," he said. "There really is a wolf in the valley, and he really is stealing the sheep. You've got to believe me."

The villagers came and looked at the boy. They shook their fingers at him. "We're smarter than you think," the people said. "This time we're just going to ignore you and your wolf! Humph!"

The shepherd boy then knew no one would believe him. He sadly walked back to his lookout. He gazed down where he always took his sheep to eat grass, but there weren't any sheep left. The wolf had taken all of them away. The boy was so sad that he began to cry.

He remembered what his parents had told him. How he wished he had listened to what they said. He wished he had just always told the truth.

He didn't want any harm to come to the sheep! Because he didn't tell the truth, no one believed him when it really mattered. Now it was too late. The shepherd boy didn't think his joke was so funny anymore.

One to Grow On

Sincerity

The shepherd boy learned the hard way about the importance of being sincere. When he played tricks on the villagers, he paid a big price for a small joke. As much fun as it is to laugh, there is also a time to be sincere.

If you were one of the villagers, would you know when to believe the shepherd boy? How do you think it felt to be tricked? What are ways you can be sure people know you are telling the truth?